# Robin Hood all at Sea

by

## Jan Mark

Illustrated by Tony Ross

You do not need to read this page –
just get on with the book!

First published in 2006 in Great Britain by
Barrington Stoke Ltd
www.barringtonstoke.co.uk

This edition based on *Robin Hood all at Sea*, published by
Barrington Stoke in 2005

ISBN 1-842994-08-5
13 digit ISBN 978-1-84299-408-5

Printed in Great Britain by Bell & Bain Ltd

## Meet The Author – Jan Mark

*What is your favourite animal?*
**The noble rat**
*What is your favourite boy's name?*
**George**
*What is your favourite girl's name?*
**Marjorie**
*What is your favourite food?*
**Pickled herring**
*What is your favourite music?*
**Klezmer**
*What is your favourite hobby?*
**Listening to music**

## Meet The Illustrator – Tony Ross

*What is your favourite animal?*
**A cat**
*What is your favourite boy's name?*
**Bill**
*What is your favourite girl's name?*
**Roxanne**
*What is your favourite food?*
**Lobster**
*What is your favourite music?*
**Irish**
*What is your favourite hobby?*
**Sailing**

# Contents

# Chapter 1
# In the Green-wood

The world is not a fair place. The rich get richer. The poor get poorer. Most of us *think* this. But Robin Hood *did* something about it.

He took money from the rich and gave it to the poor. That was fair but it was against the law and it was the rich who made the laws. Poor people said Robin Hood was a hero. Rich people called him a robber and an outlaw.

When things got too hot for Robin, he had to hide. He lived in the forest with his mates and they went on robbing the rich and giving to the poor. Now they were all outlaws.

They called the forest the Green-wood. It was a fine place to live, but sometimes it was a little too green ...

In summer the trees were green. The grass was green, the weeds were green. Even the pond was green.

Robin Hood sat under a tree. "I'm sick of all this green," he said.

His best mate, Little John, was passing by. His real name was John Little and he was very big. That was why he was called Little John. It was a joke.

"What's up with you?" said Little John.

"I'm sick of green," said Robin Hood. "Look around you, it's all green."

"Of course it is," Little John said, "that's why we call it the Green-wood."

"Well, it's too green for me," Robin said. "The trees are green, the grass is green, the weeds are green. Even I'm green."

"You should wash more often," Little John said. Robin jumped up and hit him. Little John hit Robin. They both fell in the pond. This was often the case. The other outlaws stood around looking on. Robin and Little John were dripping wet. They had slime all over them.

"Now who's green?" Robin Hood said.

"Fighting again?" Maid Marian said. "Grow up."

Maid Marian was Robin's lady friend. She was never afraid to tell him what she thought. One thing she thought was that Robin should marry her. Robin was not happy about this.

"Little John said I needed a wash," Robin told her.

"Well, now you've had one," Little John said. "So stop moaning. *You* said you were green, I didn't."

"I was talking about my clothes," Robin yelled. "Green!"

"We all wear green," Will Scarlet said. "So we can't be seen in the Green-wood."

"I know that," Robin said. "After all, it was I who told you all to wear green. But now I can't stand it any more."

"Some people don't know when they're lucky," Friar Tuck said. "We're outlaws. We do what we want, and have lots to eat and drink. We don't pay tax. We rob the rich and give the money to the poor."

"I'm sick of that too," Robin said.

"But we have to do it," Little John said. "We're outlaws." Then he added, "We could always rob the rich and keep the money."

"I'm sick of it all," Robin said. "All these people we rob – they've got more money than us."

"Yes," Marian said, "they're the rich. That's why we rob them."

"There must be better ways to earn a living," Robin said. "Look at the Sheriff of Nottingham. He's got more money than us."

"Not any more," Little John said. "We've stolen most of it."

"What about the Bishop?" Robin said.

"No. We took all his money last year," said Little John.

"The Earl?"

"No."

"Wait a bit," Friar Tuck said. "That sea captain we robbed last week. He had loads of cash."

"Not any more," Will Scarlet said. "We've got it."

"He had a fishing boat, didn't he?" Marian said.

"That's it!" Robin cried. "I'll go to sea. I'll catch fish for a living. I'll leave the Greenwood."

"Don't be silly," said Little John. "What do you know about fishing?"

"I often go fishing."

"Yes, in the pond," Little John said. "The sea's a bit bigger than our pond."

"Don't try to talk me out of it," Robin said. "I've made up my mind."

"You'll need a boat."

"I didn't hear you," Robin said. He began to hum loudly.

"Grow up," said Maid Marian. "You'll be sea-sick."

"I'm sick now," Robin said. "Didn't I tell you? I'm sick of green. The sea is blue." He sang, "Hello, blue sea! Hello, blue sky!"

"Sometimes the sea is green," Little John told him.

Robin hit him. John hit him back. They both fell in the pond.

"Here we go again," said Marian.

## Chapter 2
## To the Blue Sea

Next day Robin got ready to go. He packed all his clothes into a sack and picked up his trusty long-bow.

"You won't catch fish with a bow," Little John said. "Or are you going to hit them over the head with it?"

Robin said nothing. He just went on packing his things. He picked up his arrows.

"What are you going to do, shoot the fish?" Friar Tuck said. "They don't stay still, you know."

Robin hummed loudly. "I didn't hear you," he said.

"Grow up," said Maid Marian.

The outlaws went a little way with Robin to see him off. They stood and waved as he walked away under the trees. He waved back, but he did not turn round.

They could hear him singing.

"Hey-diddly-dee, a sailor's life for me!"

"He'll be back in a week," Little John said.

"It'll take him a week to get there," Will Scarlet said.

"OK," Little John said, "two weeks."

"Two weeks and a day, then," Will said. "One week to get there, one week to come back, and one day in the middle, catching fish."

"One day in the middle *not* catching fish," Little John said.

Then the outlaws all made bets. Marian bet that Robin would be back by the next day.

*Now what shall we do?* they all thought. When Robin was there he gave them their orders. In the end they went out and robbed the Sheriff of Nottingham, just for fun.

Robin walked on and on across fields and past farms. He had left the forest far behind him. But everything was still too green.

It took him six days to get to the sea. At night he slept in barns and sheds. He went to the door of the farms and asked for something to eat.

People said, "Who are you?"

"Robin Hood," said Robin.

*No, he's not,* people thought. But they gave him something to eat anyway, just in case.

"Where are your outlaws then?" some of them said.

"Oh, I left them at home," Robin told them.

"You aren't going to rob me, are you?" said one old woman.

"Madam, I rob the rich and give to the poor," Robin told her. "I never rob poor people."

"Are you calling me poor?" the old woman yelled. "Cheek!" And she threw a turnip at him.

"People around here don't understand me," Robin said to himself. He ate the turnip.

One morning he crossed a field and found himself on top of a cliff. The sea lay below him. It was blue.

"At last!" Robin yelled. "No more green!"

He stood on the edge of the cliff. The sea was a long way down. The beach was a long way down. At the end of the beach was a little town and there were some boats on the sand. Fishing boats.

"Hey-diddly-dee!" Robin sang. He began to walk down the cliff path. He sniffed the salt sea air as he went.

He skipped along the beach. The sand got into his boots but he didn't care. The sand was yellow, the cliff was white, the sea was blue. There was no green anywhere.

"This is bliss!" he said.

A man walked past him along the beach.

"No, mate," he said. "This is not bliss. It's the North Sea."

"Are you a fisher-man?" Robin said.

"Do I look like one?" the man said, and went on walking along the beach.

On the way into the town Robin passed the church. He looked at the grave-stones round the church.

They had writing on them. They said things like

### HERE LIES JAMES THE BAKER

and ...

### HERE LIES MARY THE COOK

and ...

## UNDER THIS STONE LIES
## HENRY THE CARPENTER

There were no fisher-men's graves. Why not?

Someone else was walking past the church. It was the man Robin had met on the beach.

"You still here?" the man said.

"Where are the fisher-men's graves?" Robin asked. "Don't fisher-men die in this town?"

The man looked at him. "No, they don't," he said. "They die at sea. Their bodies are out there, under the waves."

# Chapter 3
# In the Dark Night

Robin walked on very fast and went into the town. It didn't look like a place with much money in it.

He went down to the beach to see the fishing boats.

The fisher-men were rather rude to him.

"What are you hanging about here for?" one of them said.

"Do you need any help?" Robin said.

"What can you do?" said the fisher-man.

*I am very good at shooting arrows,* Robin thought. *I can chase deer and catch them. I can hunt rabbits. I can rob the Sheriff of Nottingham.*

"I can do anything," he said.

"Can you join two ropes?" the fisher-man asked.

"Er – no," said Robin.

"Can you put up a sail?"

"No."

"Then you're no good to me," the fisher-man said.

It was the same at the next boat, and the next. No-one wanted to give him a job.

There were big waves on the sea now, and it was getting dark. Robin didn't want to sleep in a barn or a shed. He wished he was back in the Green-wood.

*It doesn't look so green in the dark*, he thought.

Just then a woman came down the lane. She had a big basket on one arm and a baby on the other. Three little children walked behind her.

Robin Hood knew what he had to do.

"May I carry your basket?" he asked.

"It's very kind of you to offer, but I live just here," the woman said. "But could you open the gate for me?"

Robin opened the garden gate.

"You don't live in this town, do you?" the woman said. "I haven't seen you before."

"I came here to find work," Robin said. "But I have had no luck so far. Now I'm looking for a place to sleep."

"I can rent you a room," the woman said, "and I may be able to give you a job. Come on in."

Robin opened the door for the woman and they all went into the house.

"What sort of work can you do?" the woman asked.

"I'm a fisher-man," Robin said. He thought, *She's a woman. She won't know much about fishing.*

"You're just the man I'm looking for," the woman said. "My husband was a fisher-man. He died last year, but I still have his

24

boat. I rent it to some other fisher-men. You look very fit and strong. I'll tell them to give you work. Now, come and sit by the fire. We'll have supper when the children are in bed."

Robin and the fisher-man's widow sat by the fire and talked. She asked him what his name was. He didn't tell her he was Robin Hood. She might not want to have an outlaw in her house and on her boat.

"My name is Simon Wise," he said.

This was a lie. But if you're an outlaw, you don't always tell the truth.

"Well, Simon, I like the look of you," the widow said. "Can you join two ropes?"

"I can," said Robin.

That was another lie.

"Can you put up a sail?"

"I can."

Another lie.

"Can you catch fish with a hook and line?"

"I can."

Well, that was true. He'd fished in the green pond back in the Green-wood.

"Then you can sleep in my house tonight," the widow said. "In the morning we'll go and look at my boat. I'll tell the captain to give you a job."

Robin went to bed. *That was a lot of lies*, he thought. He had never joined two ropes. He had never put up a sail. He had never even been in a boat. The green pond in the Green-wood was the only water he knew.

Next day he was going to sail on the North Sea. He thought about the grave-stones round the church. He thought about the man he'd met there and what the man had said.

"Fisher-men die at sea."

I wish I was back in the Green-Wood

28

# Chapter 4
# Under Grey Clouds

In the morning the widow took Robin down to the beach to see her boat. She picked up the baby and the three little children ran behind her. Robin picked up his bow and arrows, as he always did.

"What are those?" the children asked.

"Where I come from, we use them to catch fish," Robin told them. That was another lie.

There was a lot of wind and the waves were still very big but the sun was shining.

"This is the boat," the widow said.

Robin had seen this boat before.

"And this is the Captain," the widow went on.

Robin had seen the Captain before too. And the Captain had seen him.

"This is Simon Wise," the widow said.

The Captain looked at Robin.

"I want you to give him a job," the widow said. "He can join a rope and put up a sail and catch a fish on a hook as well as any of you."

"Can he?" the Captain said. "Are you sure?" He gave Robin an angry look. "You didn't know all that yesterday."

"Now, do it to please me," the widow said. "You know you need another man."

"Well, I'll do what you ask me," the Captain said. But he didn't look happy.

"Good luck," the widow said, and went back to her house with the children.

"Now, what lies have you been telling her?" the Captain said.

"Let me work on your boat," Robin said. "You won't be sorry."

"I'm sorry already," the Captain said. He looked on as Robin got into the boat.

Robin tripped over his long-bow and fell flat on the deck.

"You're just a silly great lump who
knows nothing about boats," said the
Captain. "And put that bow out of the way
where you can't trip over it."

"How did that woman's husband die?"
Robin asked.

"He went over the side," the Captain said. "It was a windy day, like this. And a wild sea, like this."

*That's why there are no fisher-men's graves*, thought Robin. And that man he had met. What had he said?

"Fisher-men die at sea."

The rest of the men had begun to laugh when they saw Robin fall into the boat. And they went on laughing.

The men pulled up the anchor and put up the sail. The boat rocked and rolled over the waves. The land was now far away. The beach, then the town and then even the cliffs had all gone. There was nothing all around them but grey sea and grey sky.

The men put worms on their hooks and fished over the side of the boat. Robin put a worm on his hook and looked over the side.

The wind blew, the waves rolled up and down, the boat rocked. The men were catching fish. Robin was being sick.

This went on all morning. By noon a heap of shining fish lay on the deck. Robin also lay on the deck. He was greener than he had ever been back in the Green-wood.

The Captain stepped over him. He did not look at Robin but he spoke in a loud voice.

"On this boat," he said, "we share everything. We share our food, we share our drink and we share our fish. But we only share our fish," he went on, "if we catch any fish to share."

"Give me time," Robin said with a groan. "I'm not used to this boat yet. It goes up and down."

"You'd better get used to it," the Captain said. "All boats go up and down."

The crew laughed and put more worms on their hooks. Robin hadn't got a fish yet so his hook still had the same old worm on it. He held it over the side. The worm was very dead. Fish looked at it and swam away.

*The outlaws were right, Robin thought. What am I doing? These fisher-men think I'm a fool, and I am a fool. I just wish I could take them all home to the Green-wood. Then they'd see what kind of a man I am. They'd see me when I'm shooting arrows and chasing deer and fighting Little John and robbing the Sheriff of Nottingham.*

But the fisher-men didn't know that he was Robin Hood. They thought he was Simon Wise.

When they called him Simon he forgot to reply. He was too busy being sick. That made them laugh all the more.

"Doesn't even know his own name," they said.

Then a shout went up.

"A sail! A sail!"

They saw a dark shape coming towards them. Another shout went up.

"It's a Frenchman!"

The dark shape came closer. It was sailing very fast.

"Pirates!"

# Chapter 5
# The Black Sail

The pirate ship looked evil. It had a black sail. The men on the deck looked evil. The sun shone on their swords.

"We're all lost," the Captain said. "They'll take our fish and they'll take our boat. They'll take us back to France in chains and put us in prison."

"Well, what are you going to do about it?" Robin said. He sat up. Now he didn't feel sick any more.

"Do about it?" the Captain yelled. "What can we do about it? Look at those pirates. They've got sharp swords. Their ship is ten times faster than our boat. They'll run us down, and jump aboard our boat. What can we fight them with? Fish hooks? Worms?"

Robin sprang up. He picked up his bow and grabbed an arrow.

"Don't be scared," he cried. "Let them come closer and then we'll see who will win this fight."

"Put that down," the Captain said, "and shut up. You'll hurt someone. We're sick of all your big words."

Robin lifted his bow and let the arrow
fly. But just at that moment, a huge wave
hit the boat and the arrow went high up in
the air. Everyone forgot about the pirates
and stood looking at it.

After a bit it came down again and hit
the deck, not far from where the Captain
was standing.

"Whose side are you on?" the Captain yelled. The arrow was stuck in the deck.

Robin swore. He tugged the arrow from the deck and grabbed a rope that was lying near it. Then he tied himself to the mast.

"We should have done that ages ago," the Captain said. "It would have saved us a lot of bother."

But now Robin could stay on his feet however much the boat rocked and rolled. The other ship was very close now. The fisher-men could see the pirates, armed to the teeth.

Robin bent his bow again and let fly with another arrow. This one flew across the water and found its target in a pirate's heart.

The pirate gave a cry, threw up his arms and was gone. The other pirates yelled and waved their swords, but the swords were no good to them and they knew it. Twenty pirates with swords could do nothing against one man with a long-bow.

The fisher-men cheered.

"Bet you can't do that twice," the Captain said.

Robin shot another arrow and a second pirate fell dead. Then another and another. One by one the pirates fell dead. They hung over the side of their ship.

At last only the pirate Captain was left. He waved his sword and flashed his teeth.

"You'll never take me alive!" he cried.

"We don't want to take you alive," Robin said, and shot his last arrow. It zipped from the bow, hissed across the water and hit the pirate Captain with a dull thud.

The fisher-men cheered again and waved their hats in the air. The Captain shook Robin by the hand.

"I knew you were a brave fighter as soon as I saw you," he said.

"Did you?" said Robin.

By now the pirate ship was sailing close to the fishing boat.

"Change tack!" the Captain yelled. "We don't want the pirate ship to ram into us. Head for land. Our boat is safe. Our fish are safe, thanks to Simon."

"Hooray for Simon!" the fisher-men cheered. "Simon shall share our fish."

This time Robin Hood didn't forget that he was Simon Wise. He gave a little bow and turned to the Captain with a modest smile.

"Forget about the fish," he said. "What about the ship? You're not just going to sail away from it, are you?"

"Well, I suppose we could tow it home," the Captain said. "Maybe we can sell it."

"Well, what kind of a ship is it?" Robin said.

"It's a pirate ship," the fisher-men told him.

"And what do pirates do?" Robin asked them.

The fisher-men shook their heads. "They steal from honest men like us."

"So what will they have on their ship?"

The fisher-men looked at each other.

"Fish!"

"No," Robin said, "I don't think so. They also steal from rich sea captains. I've done it myself," he added. "Let's get on board the ship and see what we can find. Follow me, boys!" he yelled. "This is what I'm good at."

# Chapter 6
# The Golden Prize

As soon as they got close to the pirate ship, Robin jumped on board. The fishermen followed.

First they threw the dead pirates into the sea. They were in the way.

Robin pulled out his trusty dagger and went down into the cabin. He wanted to be sure that there were no pirates still hiding in there. Then he led the way into the hold. This was a dark place in the bottom of the ship where the pirates kept their treasure.

"Bring a light!" he yelled. The Captain came in with a lantern. The fisher-men were right behind him. They stood there with their mouths open.

There were great sea chests all around them, with huge metal locks. Huge sacks lay in the corners of the hold. They clinked when people kicked them.

"Bring it all up on deck," Robin said. "Then we'll be able to see what we're doing."

The fisher-men carried the sacks and chests up onto the deck. Robin slit open the sacks with his dagger. The Captain found an axe and chopped the lids off the chests.

The sacks were full of jewels. Gold rings and necklaces and bracelets fell out onto the deck. There was even a king's crown in one of the sacks.

"These were high-class pirates," the Captain said.

The chests were filled with coins.

Everyone sat around staring. They had never seen so much money in all their lives.

"What shall we do with it all?" one of them said.

"I'll tell you what," Robin said, "we'll share it. You lot can keep one half and I'll give the rest to the widow and her children. If she hadn't given me a job on this boat we'd never have found the treasure."

"Wait a bit," the Captain said. "That's not fair. If the widow hadn't given you a job you would never have sailed with us. But if you hadn't sailed with us we'd be dead men by now, or in prison. You won this treasure all by yourself. You keep the lot."

Robin thought about it.

"That's true," he said. "I'll tell you what. You take the ship and sell it and keep the money. I'll have the treasure. I will give half to the widow and her children, and keep the rest. Then I'll give it to the poor. Those pirates robbed the rich. It's only fair if the poor get the money they stole."

"You sound like Robin Hood," the Captain said. "Robbing the rich and giving to the poor. That's what Robin Hood does."

"How do you know about Robin Hood?" Robin said.

"Everyone knows about Robin Hood," the Captain said. "He's famous all over England. I'd like to shake his hand."

Robin thought about this on the way back to land. He sat on the deck of the pirate ship with the treasure all around him. He was choosing some rings and a necklace for Maid Marian.

*Shall I tell them the truth?* he thought. *Shall I tell them that Simon Wise is really Robin Hood? I think they'd like to know. The Captain wanted to shake my hand.*

Then he thought again.

*Yes, everyone knows Robin Hood. He's famous all over England. He's famous for chasing deer. He's famous for shooting arrows. He's famous for robbing the rich and giving to the poor. But he's not famous for being sea-sick. And the Captain has shaken the hand of Robin Hood already, even if he doesn't know it.*

So he said nothing.

When the fishing boat got to land, everyone in the town was on the beach to greet them. First the fisher-men took the fish off the boat.

Then they took off the pirate treasure. A great cheer went up from one end of the beach to the other as the men carried the sacks and chests ashore.

Robin went over to the widow who was waiting with her children.

"Madam," he said, "half of all this is yours. You took pity on Simon Wise when he was down on his luck. Now you will never be poor again."

"And what will you do?" the widow said. "You're a rich man, now."

55

"I shall give everything to the poor," Robin said. "I don't want to be rich. Rich men get robbed. I know all about that. And now I must go back to where I came from," he said. "My friends will be missing me."

He hoped that his friends were missing him.

Next morning he set out to buy a horse and a donkey. He loaded his half of the treasure onto the donkey and rode the horse. Then he said good-bye to the widow and her children. He said good-bye to the fisher-men and shook hands again with the Captain. Then he rode up the path to the top of the cliff.

The grey North Sea lay behind him, under a grey sky. The salt sea wind blew down his neck. Ahead of him lay green fields, green grass, and the Green-wood.

He rode towards it and never looked
back.